The Secret of the
EAGLE FEATHERS

Story by Maura Elizabeth Keleher McKinley
Illustrations by Craig Brown

RSVP
RAINTREE
STECK-VAUGHN
PUBLISHERS
The Steck-Vaughn Company

To my grandparents, who are wise and wonderful. — M.E.K.M.

To Max and Moe: Best Friends. — C.B.

Publish-a-Book is a trademark of Steck-Vaughn Company.

Printed in the United States of America.

1 2 3 4 5 6 7 8 9 0 IP 01 00 99 98 97 96

Library of Congress Cataloging-in-Publication Data

McKinley, Maura Elizabeth Keleher, 1986 –
    The secret of the eagle feathers / story by Maura Elizabeth Keleher McKinley ;
illustrations by Craig Brown.
      p.   cm. — (Publish-a-book)
    Summary: An Indian girl follows her grandfather's instructions and, with the help of an eagle and a coyote, manages to find his stolen headdress and learn the secret that has made him a great leader.
    ISBN 0–8172–4436–0
    1. Indians of North America — Juvenile fiction.   2. Children's writings, American.   [1. Indians of North America — Fiction.   2. Grandfathers — Fiction.   3. Children's writings.]   I. Brown, Craig McFarland, ill. II. Title. III. Series.
PZ7.M4786785Se   1997
[Fic] — dc21
                                                        96-44250
                                                         CIP   AC

Owanee lived with her grandfather on the shores of Loon Lake. One day while Owanee was picking berries, she heard a shout. She ran to see what was wrong. When she got to her tepee, she saw a boat leaving. In it was a man with her grandfather's most prized possession, his Indian chief headdress.

5

Owanee looked all around, but her grandfather was nowhere to be seen. Then she heard a muffled voice coming from the tepee. Owanee dashed inside. There she found Grandfather, bound and gagged. She quickly took off his gag and, with great effort, untied the ropes that bound him.

"Grandfather, what happened?" Owanee asked.

"I was sitting in the tepee when all of a sudden my lost brother came in. He had been to the land of the Great Mountains and learned the secret that made me chief. The next thing I knew, I was tied and gagged," said Grandfather. Then he surprised her by saying, "I must go to the spirit who makes the day bright."

"But Grandfather, why? What is the secret? Can I go instead of you?" asked Owanee.

Grandfather sighed and looked proudly at his strong, brave granddaughter. He knew she was ready for an adventure, and that she would be protected by his many animal friends.

"Yes, Owanee, but you must be careful."

9

"What must I do?" asked Owanee.

"First, you must make a sturdy canoe. Then you must cross Loon Lake. Be careful! When you get to the far shore there will be an eagle waiting. Climb on her back and whisper these words into her ear:

*Oh brave eagle, soar over the plains
until you get to high mountains.
Take me over the first mountain.*

"On your journey you will find a coyote. Whisper these words into his ear: *Oh tricky coyote, take me over these two mountains on your fast legs.* Then climb on his back. When you get to the foot of the fourth mountain, there will be a bead necklace circling a rock. The necklace will give you strength to climb this mountain by yourself. At the top of that mountain you will find a spirit. She will tell you the secret."

Owanee followed her grandfather's instructions, and soon found herself on the back of a magnificent eagle. Owanee could feel the wind rush through her unbraided hair. She felt free and wild just like the eagle.

Suddenly, the eagle turned her head around sharply. Owanee shrieked in surprise. Behind them was a man riding a vulture. He grabbed Owanee and pulled her onto the vulture. Instantly, the eagle rammed into the vulture, throwing both its riders off. The eagle swooped under Owanee and caught her before she had fallen too far.

The soft glide of the eagle kept her
safe until they were over the first mountain.
Owanee gave the eagle a big hug and
whispered, "Thank you." The eagle gave
Owanee four feathers for a remembrance.

Owanee looked all around. She heard a rustle in the bushes, and out came a coyote. When he walked up to Owanee and licked her, she knew this was the right one. She whispered the words her grandfather had told her and climbed onto the coyote's back. They started up the mountain, which was very tall and dangerous.

"Hold on tightly," the coyote called to Owanee. Owanee was tired and scared. She began to wonder whether she would have the strength to complete her journey.

When they reached the top of the mountain, the coyote and Owanee rested. Owanee dreamed about the man she had seen on the vulture. She saw him push her and the coyote down the mountain. Then she heard him say, "You had better not go to the spirit who makes the day bright. Or ELSE!"

She woke up and told the coyote of her dream. The coyote seemed surprised. "I had the same dream," he said.

At the bottom of the last mountain Owanee found the beaded necklace and started climbing. When she was halfway up, a rock slide carried her all the way down again. Her clothes were badly ripped and her skin was scratched. When she caught her breath, she started climbing again. This time the same man appeared and pushed her down. Down and down she fell! Luckily for her, she landed in a stream. Exhausted, she tried again, and this time she made it to the top.

The spirit was waiting for her. She had hair
as black as ebony, eyes as dark as a raven, and skin
the color of copper. She smelled as fresh and sweet
as spring. In her hair was a crown of bluebells.

Owanee was frightened and excited at the same
time. She said in a humble voice, "I am looking for
my grandfather's headdress and the secret that
made him chief."

The spirit answered in a lovely tone, "In the cave behind me the bad man is being held prisoner. He will bother you no more. Here is your grandfather's headdress. I will whisper the secret to you now:

Whoever can get four feathers from an eagle without killing it will have good luck the rest of his or her life. But if that person tells anyone the secret, all will be lost."

29

The next thing Owanee knew, she was back
at home handing the headdress to her grandfather.
He was very, very proud of her.

Owanee grew up to have as much wisdom
and courage as her grandfather, and she became
a leader of her people.

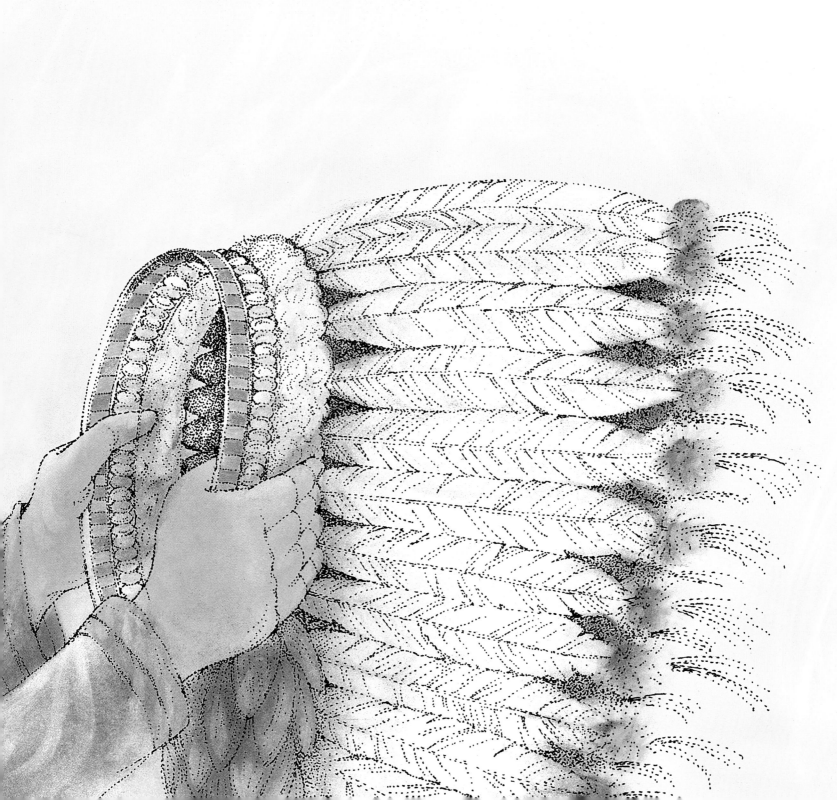

Lee Ira Siegman, Ltd. Photography

Maura Elizabeth Keleher McKinley, author of **The Secret of the Eagle Feathers**, is ten years old and lives in Whitefish Bay, Wisconsin, with her mom and dad, her eight-year-old brother, Michael, her two-year-old sister, Clare, and her two cats, Jack and Houston. She was in fourth grade at Cumberland Elementary School when she wrote *The Secret of the Eagle Feathers* for a writing workshop taught by Mrs. Jude Schulze. It was Mrs. Schulze who encouraged Maura to enter the 1996 Publish-a-Book™ Contest. This is the second writing contest Maura has won. When she was in third grade, her teacher, Mrs. Anne Brooks, suggested that Maura enter a local writing contest. Maura wrote a story for that contest and won first prize in her age group.

Maura has always loved stories. She reads every day, and often has to be reminded to put her book down at the dinner table. When she was younger, she eagerly listened to stories told by her parents, aunts, and uncles. She always found ways to get them to tell "one more story." She still listens to their stories, but now she has begun telling stories of her own to her little sister.

Maura became interested in Native Americans during camping trips her family took to Lake Superior, to the mountains, and to the Southwest. She has read many tales by or about Native Americans, and she is impressed with their respect for nature and animals. Maura loves the outdoors, too. She likes climbing trees and rocks and searching for insects and small animals. She often finds secret spots of her own under trees or in bushes.

Maura also loves music and dance. She has been playing the violin since she was six years old. She hopes to be able to play Irish fiddle music before too long and to learn Irish dancing. She is also an enthusiastic soccer player. In addition, Maura loves to act. She recently performed in the First Stage Milwaukee production of *The Best Christmas Pageant Ever*.

The twenty honorable-mention winners in the **1996 Raintree/Steck-Vaughn Publish-a-Book™ Contest** were Amy Anderson, Joyce Kilmer School, Milltown, New Jersey; Meghan Codd, Riffenburgh Elementary School, Fort Collins, Colorado; Jonathan Cantwell, Ramblewood Elementary School, Coral Springs, Florida; Christopher Riedel, Haycock Elementary School, Falls Church, Virginia; Jonathan Jans, Jack Hille School, Oak Forest, Illinois; Kevin P. Barry, John Pettibone School, New Milford, Connecticut; Hiram Lew, St. Thomas Apostle School, San Francisco, California; Becky Kuplin, Sussex County Eastern District Library, Franklin, New Jersey; Amanda Marchetti, St. Joseph Memorial School, Hazleton, Pennsylvania; Julia K. Corley, Ruby Ray Swift Elementary School, Arlington, Texas; Sally Rees, Richards Elementary School, Whitefish Bay, Wisconsin; Katherine Connors, Haycock Elementary School, Falls Church, Virginia; Amanda R. Simpson, Mitchell Elementary School, Mitchell, Nebraska; Sarah Wexelbaum, Pine Crest School, Boca Raton, Florida; Matthew Ports, Hope Christian School, Albuquerque, New Mexico; Bridget Taylor, St. Anne's School, Bethlehem, Pennsylvania; Hillary Birtley, Clark Elementary School, St. Louis, Missouri; Chris Morin, Boulan Park Middle School, Troy, Michigan; Lauren Ferris, St. Vincent's Elementary School, Petaluma, California; Rula Assi, Juniper School, Escondido, California.

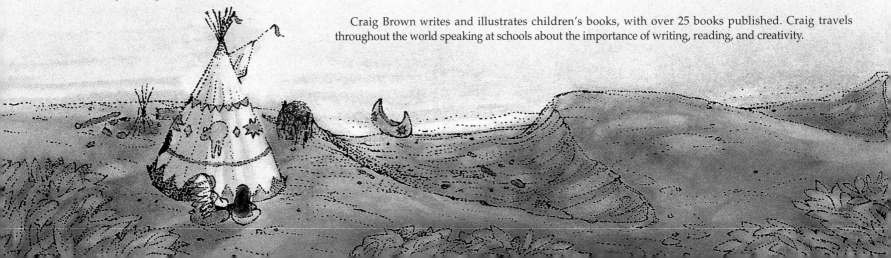

Craig Brown writes and illustrates children's books, with over 25 books published. Craig travels throughout the world speaking at schools about the importance of writing, reading, and creativity.